THE YUCKIEST, STINKIEST, BEST VALENTINE EVER

BY BRENDA A. FERBER
PICTURES BY TEDD ARNOLD

DIAL BOOKS FOR YOUNG READERS
an imprint of Penguin Group (USA) Inc.

FOR JACOB AND SAMMY, WHO ARE NEITHER YUCKY NOR STINKY.
I LOVE YOU BOTH! XOXO MOM
—B.A.F.

FOR OWEN, WITH HEARTS
—T.A.

DIAL BOOKS FOR YOUNG READERS
A DIVISION OF PENGUIN YOUNG READERS GROUP
PUBLISHED BY THE PENGUIN GROUP
PENGUIN GROUP (USA) INC., 375 HUDSON STREET, NEW YORK, NY 10014, U.S.A.

PENGUIN GROUP (CANADA), 90 EGLINTON AVENUE EAST, SUITE 700, TORONTO, ONTARIO, CANADA M4P 2Y3 (A DIVISION OF PEARSON PENGUIN CANADA INC.) • PENGUIN BOOKS LTD, 80 STRAND, LONDON WC2R ORL, ENGLAND • PENGUIN IRELAND, 25 ST. STEPHEN'S GREEN, DUBLIN 2, IRELAND (A DIVISION OF PENGUIN BOOKS LTD) • PENGUIN GROUP (AUSTRALIA), 250 CAMBERWELL ROAD, CAMBERWELL, VICTORIA 3124, AUSTRALIA (A DIVISION OF PEARSON AUSTRALIA GROUP PTY LTD) • PENGUIN BOOKS INDIA PVT LTD, 11 COMMUNITY CENTRE, PANCHSHEEL PARK, NEW DELHI - 110 017, INDIA • PENGUIN GROUP (NZ), 67 APOLLO DRIVE, ROSEDALE, AUCKLAND 0632, NEW ZEALAND (A DIVISION OF PEARSON NEW ZEALAND LTD) • PENGUIN BOOKS (SOUTH AFRICA) (PTY) LTD, 24 STURDEE AVENUE, ROSEBANK, JOHANNESBURG 2196, SOUTH AFRICA • PENGUIN BOOKS LTD, REGISTERED OFFICES: 80 STRAND, LONDON WC2R ORL, ENGLAND

DESIGNED BY NANCY R. LEO-KELLY
TEXT SET IN ASHCAN BB
MANUFACTURED IN CHINA ON ACID-FREE PAPER
1 3 5 7 9 10 8 6 4 2

LIBRARY OF CONGRESS CATALOGING-IN-PUBLICATION DATA
FERBER, BRENDA A.
THE YUCKIEST, STINKIEST, BEST VALENTINE EVER / BY BRENDA A. FERBER ; PICTURES BY TEDD ARNOLD.
P. CM.
SUMMARY: A YOUNG BOY NAMED LEON PURSUES A RUNAWAY VALENTINE MEANT FOR HIS TRUE LOVE, ZOEY MALONEY.
ISBN 978-0-8037-3505-7 (HARDCOVER)
[1. VALENTINE'S DAY—FICTION. 2. LOVE—FICTION.] I. ARNOLD, TEDD, ILL. II. TITLE.
PZ7.F3543YU 2012 [E]—DC23 2011047668

THE IMAGES IN THIS BOOK WERE DONE DIGITALLY, USING A STYLUS ON A WACOM CINTIQ MONITOR.

LEON HAD A CRUSH. A SECRET CRUSH. A DREAMY CRUSH. A LET-HER-CUT-IN-LINE-AT-THE-WATER-FOUNTAIN CRUSH. AND TODAY LEON PLANNED TO PROCLAIM HIS LOVE. IT WOULD BE THE BEST VALENTINE'S DAY **EVER!**

LEON CUT A BIG RED HEART OUT OF CONSTRUCTION PAPER. HE ADDED ARMS, LEGS, AND A FACE. WHAT A SWEET VALENTINE! HE TURNED IT OVER AND WROTE:
Dear Zoey Maloney,
I love you!
Love,
Leon
GLUE

BUT WHEN LEON TRIED TO PUT IT INTO AN ENVELOPE, THE VALENTINE JUMPED OUT OF HIS HANDS.
PUL-EESE! YOU CAN'T TELL ZOEY MALONEY YOU LOVE HER!

I CAN'T? WHY NOT?
IT'S DISGUSTING, THAT'S WHY NOT. IT'S MUSHY AND GROSS AND JUST PLAIN YUCKY!

BUT I THOUGHT VALENTINE'S DAY WAS ALL ABOUT **LOVE**.

HA! VALENTINE'S DAY IS ALL ABOUT CANDY. I'M TALKIN' CANDY HEARTS, CHOCOLATES, CARAMELS, **THE WORKS!**

HONEY B
B MINE

AND WITH THAT, THE VALENTINE LEAPED OUT THE WINDOW AND RAN AWAY.
WAIT! COME BACK!
BUT THE VALENTINE RAN FASTER, CALLING—
LOVE IS YUCKY. STINKY TOO. IT WILL TURN YOUR BRAIN TO GOO!

DOWN THE ROAD RAN THE VALENTINE. AFTER HIM RAN LEON.

THEY CAME TO A PLAYGROUND WHERE SOME BOYS WERE PLAYING BASKETBALL.
HELP! LEON WANTS TO GIVE ME TO HIS SECRET CRUSH!

EEW!
SAID THE BIGGEST BOY.
GRRROSS!
SAID THE MIDDLE-SIZED BOY.
COOTIES!
SAID THE LITTLEST BOY.

YOU DON'T UNDERSTAND. ZOEY MALONEY IS MY ONE TRUE LOVE.
PIPE DOWN! YOU GIVE ME TO ZOEY MALONEY AND WE'LL BE THE LAUGHINGSTOCK OF THE WHOLE SCHOOL!

AND ON E RAN, CALLING—
LOVE IS YUCKY. STINKY TOO. IT WILL TURN YOUR BRAIN TO GOO!

THROUGH THE PARK RAN THE VALENTINE.

AFTER HIM RAN LEON, AND THE BOYS, WHO WERE CHEERING **WILDLY** FOR THE VALENTINE'S ESCAPE.

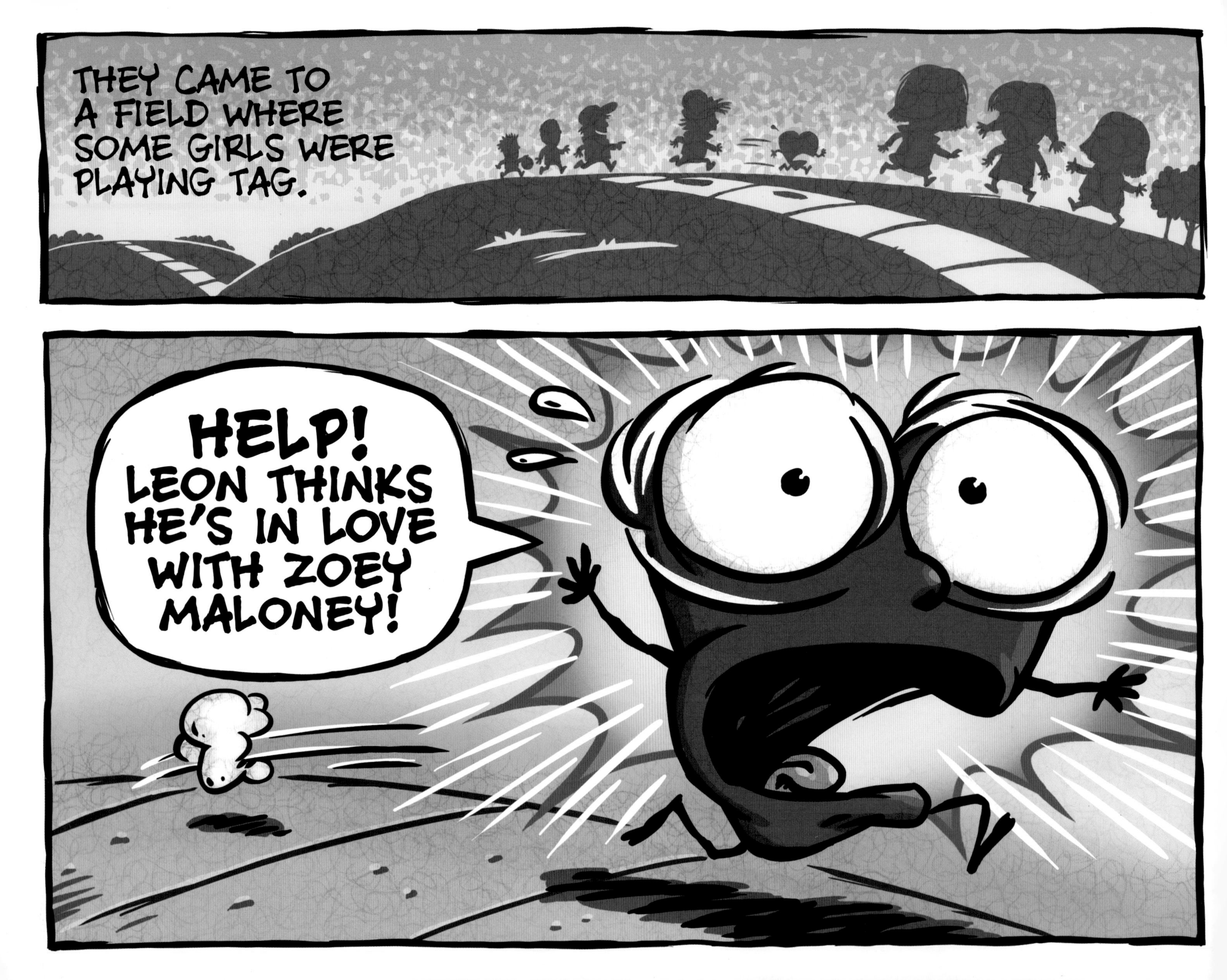
THEY CAME TO A FIELD WHERE SOME GIRLS WERE PLAYING TAG.
HELP! LEON THINKS HE'S IN LOVE WITH ZOEY MALONEY!

HOW CUTE!
SAID THE BIGGEST GIRL.
HOW ADORABLE!
SAID THE MIDDLE-SIZED GIRL.
HOW ROMANTIC!
SAID THE LITTLEST GIRL.

BUT DOES ZOEY MALONEY LOVE YOU BACK?
LEON FROZE. HE HAD NO IDEA. SHE HAD PICKED HIM TO BE ON HER KICKBALL TEAM ONCE. WAS THAT LOVE?
ZOEY MALONEY DOES LOVE ME. I THINK.

THE VALENTINE SHOOK HIS HEAD.
LOVE IS NOTHIN' BUT TROUBLE, KID!
STICK WITH CANDY. IT'S A SURE THING!

AND ON HE RAN, CALLING—
LOVE IS YUCKY. STINKY TOO. IT WILL TURN YOUR BRAIN TO GOO!

INTO TOWN RAN THE VALENTINE. AFTER HIM RAN LEON, THE BOYS, AND THE GIRLS, WHO WERE HOPING TO SEE **TRUE LOVE** TRIUMPH.

THEY CAME TO A FOUNTAIN WHERE SOME TEENAGERS WERE HANGING OUT.
HELP! LEON WANTS TO GIVE ME TO ZOEY MALONEY, AND HE'S NOT EVEN SURE SHE LOVES HIM BACK!

THAT'S BOLD!
SAID THE BIGGEST TEEN.
THAT'S RISKY!
SAID THE MIDDLE-SIZED TEEN.
THAT'S NOTHING!
SAID THE LITTLEST TEEN.
I CAN FIND OUT IF ZOEY MALONEY LIKES HIM. MY BROTHER IS BEST FRIENDS WITH SAM SAMUELSON, WHOSE COUSIN IS RILEY RICHARDS, WHO LIVES NEXT DOOR TO LINDSEY LEWIS, WHO PLAYS ON THE SAME SOCCER

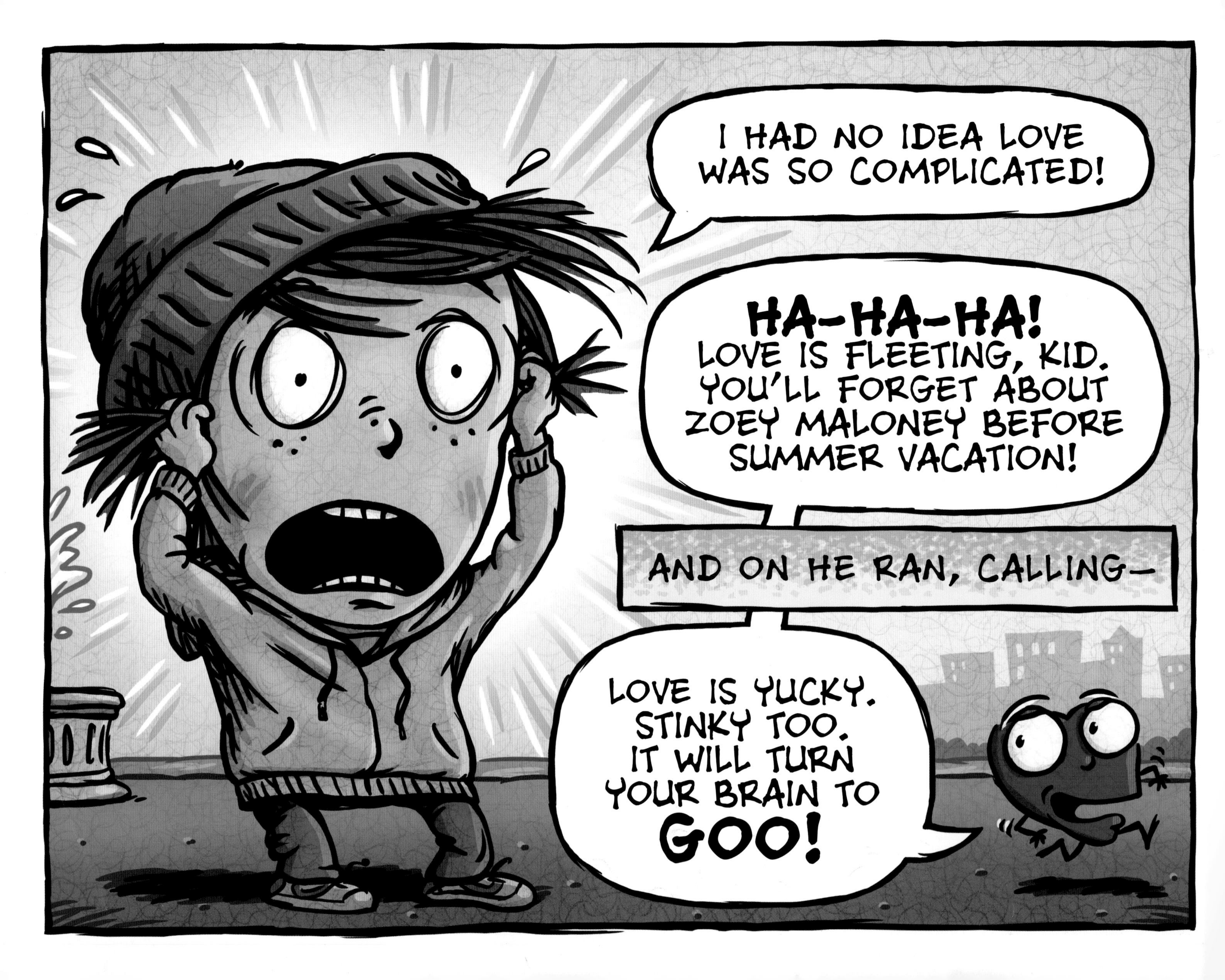
I HAD NO IDEA LOVE WAS SO COMPLICATED!
HA-HA-HA! LOVE IS FLEETING, KID. YOU'LL FORGET ABOUT ZOEY MALONEY BEFORE SUMMER VACATION!
AND ON HE RAN, CALLING—
LOVE IS YUCKY. STINKY TOO. IT WILL TURN YOUR BRAIN TO GOO!

AROUND THE CORNER RAN THE VALENTINE.

AFTER HIM RAN LEON, THE BOYS, THE GIRLS, AND THE TEENS, WHO WERE CURIOUS TO SEE HOW THIS WHOLE **MESS** WOULD TURN OUT.

THE VALENTINE DASHED INSIDE SUGARMAN'S CANDY SHOP...
Sugarman'
CANDY SHO
...WHERE HE SLAMMED INTO A GIRL WITH HAIR SLEEK AS SUNSHINE, EYES BRIGHT AS THE OCEAN, AND FRECKLES LIKE PERFECT SPECKS OF SAND...
SWEETS LOVE
GUMMIES
CHOCOLA

ZOEY MALONEY!
ZOEY MALONEY LOOKED AT LEON. THEN SHE LOOKED AT THE VALENTINE. LEON HELD HIS BREATH.
TO LEON

A SMILE SPREAD ACROSS ZOEY MALONEY'S FACE. LEON'S HEART SOARED.
JUST THEN, THE VALENTINE NOTICED ZOEY MALONEY'S VALENTINE.
SWEET!
LOVE U
B MINE
ZOEY MALONEY'S VALENTINE GIGGLED.

THE BOYS SAID—
WHOA!
THE GIRLS SAID—
OHH!
THE TEENAGERS SAID—
WAY TO GO!

HEY, YOU'RE IN LOVE TOO!
AT LAST, THE VALENTINE WAS SPEECHLESS.
LOVE U
B MINE

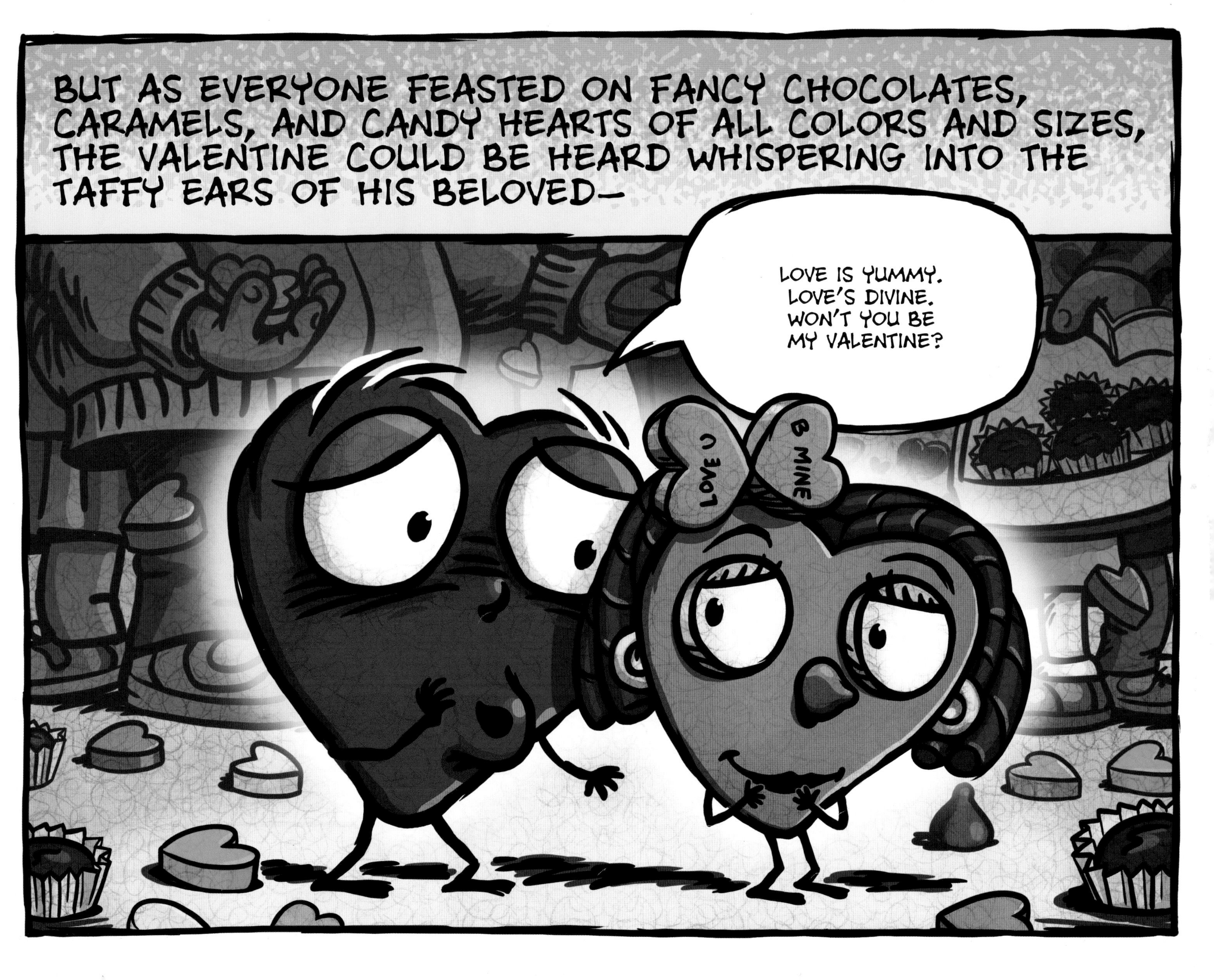
BUT AS EVERYONE FEASTED ON FANCY CHOCOLATES, CARAMELS, AND CANDY HEARTS OF ALL COLORS AND SIZES, THE VALENTINE COULD BE HEARD WHISPERING INTO THE TAFFY EARS OF HIS BELOVED—
LOVE IS YUMMY. LOVE'S DIVINE. WON'T YOU BE MY VALENTINE?
LOVE U
B MINE

THEY ALL AGREED—
IT WAS THE BEST VALENTINE'S DAY
EVER!
THE END